CW00433031

Summer of Sunshine

By Rebecca Paulinyi

1

To hear about new releases, see pictures of my dog and generally hear about my writing, you can sign up to my newsletter here: http://tiny.cc/paulinyi

This book is dedicated to my readers. Thank you to every single one of you for choosing my stories to read.

CHAPTER ONE
Lee

"We need a holiday," Lee said, running a hand through her blonde hair before remembering that there were still remnants of her daughter's meal on her fingertips.

She was sat with her husband, James, at the dinner table; a fairly standard occurrence, although with his shift work as a police officer, it didn't happen every day.

He yawned; it had been a long night shift, and despite a quick nap earlier in the day, he was ready for an early night. "Yeah?"

"Don't you think? We've not been away since our honeymoon..."

James nodded, watching as Holly fed herself quarters of strawberry, her favourite dessert.

"Well, between a two-and-a-half year old, and three careers between us, time does seem to disappear!"

Lee laughed, but it was a little hollow. He was right; time did just disappear. It was a whirl of nursery drop-offs, cafe shifts, law work, police shifts - not to mention housework, and attempting to spend some quality time together as a couple.

"But a holiday sounds nice," he said, and she wondered if he'd seen that she really needed this. She knew he was feeling almost as anxious as she was every month as it became apparent that she was not pregnant.

It had been so easy last time; too easy really. And yet now, when a second baby would complete their family so well, things seemed to be much more complicated.

"What if we suggested it to Beth and Caspian?" Lee said, sipping the tea in front of her before realising it had gone stone cold at some point during the meal. "It's so hard to see her often with her living up in Scotland. We could get cheap flights, lie on a beach somewhere or next to a pool..."

"Ask her," James said. "And then we'll try to get our schedules to all line up! Once this little monkey's in school, it won't be so easy!"

"That's years away!" Lee said, but she knew how quickly the last two and a half years had gone.

She was determined to make their schedules work. After all, Beth was currently writing full time, and surely that could be done anywhere? Lee's manager and best friend Gina was perfectly capable of having sole control over the cafe, and as she was self-employed as a lawyer, that was pretty easy to organise too. No, it would be Caspian and James that were the hard ones to organise - but if she and Beth could be flexible, she was confident they could make it work.

She really felt they could do with the break away from their everyday lives.

*　　*　　*

Although these days shifts at the cafe she owned were few and far between, the next day was one such shift - and she was working with Gina, who she definitely didn't see as often as she should. In the early days of her move to Totnes, they had worked together - and lived together - every day, and though her life was so full of joy now, sometimes Lee did miss those days. Living with Gina had been like living with a sister - they had become closer than friends, even in the very short time they flat-shared.

"I have news!" Gina shouted at her before she'd even got the door closed behind her. Gina's hair was currently purple - one of many colours it had been over the years Lee had known her and, she presumed, many others in the years before - and she was beaming at Lee.

"Good morning to you too!" she said, but she was smiling - Gina's mood was infectious. "Go on, what's the news?"

Gina flashed her left hand, and it took Lee a second to cotton on.

"Tom proposed?" she said with a gasp.

"Tom proposed!" Gina was practically shouting, and Lee dropped her handbag on the floor to give her best friend a hug.

"Congratulations!" Lee said, and although her words were lost in the hug, she was fairly sure Gina got the sentiment. "Tell me everything while we set up."

As they ground coffee, wiped surfaces and set out cakes, Gina told her how they had been for a walk on the beach when suddenly Tom had gone down on one knee and produced a ring.

"So sappy," Gina said with a roll of her eyes, but Lee knew that however sappy her friend found proposals, this one had stolen her heart.

"So romantic," Lee corrected her. "Have you set a date?"

"Not yet, it only happened the yesterday! I was going to ring, but then I thought as we were working together it would be better in person."

"Definitely better in person."

"We won't be having some big traditional do - no offence, just not my scene."

"None taken," Lee said with a laugh, as she turned the sign to 'open'.

"But whatever we do, and whenever it is - will you be my bridesmaid?"

Lee was distracted by the pinging of the bell, announcing a customer, but as Gina greeted them, she flashed her a smile. "I'd love to - but just remember I let you choose your own bridesmaid dress!"

Gina waited until the customer had sat down to chuckle at Lee's friendly reminder. While the two were good friends, their fashion taste was poles apart.

"I'll remember," she said, frothing the milk until it bubbled. "Don't panic!"

CHAPTER TWO
James

They were lucky, James thought as he surveyed the rest of the plane, that Holly tended to be a pretty laid-back toddler. He smiled sympathetically at parents trying to calm down a tiny baby, and at a mother sat with a pre-school age child who was not impressed with the fact that electronics had to be turned off. It wasn't easy, this parenting malarkey, but somehow he and Lee seemed to have muddled through all right with Holly. He did worry sometimes that they had got very lucky with such a well behaved little girl... what if a second was a nightmare?

At the back of his mind, he was even more concerned that they might not be able to have a second.

With a sigh, he pushed that from his mind. Lee was right; they did need a holiday. It had been all the serious stuff lately and none of the fun.

Holly looked excited as she swung her legs back and forth - although thankfully, they were not yet long enough to knock the chair in front and irritate them - even with the limited leg room.

"Fly!" she said, a word which she had been practising ever since they had told her they were going to go on a plane, and everyone in the surrounding seats smiled at her - although, James thought, they were probably mostly relieved she wasn't screaming.

"Soon!" he told her. "You've got to be patient..." Her first time on a plane - although he doubted she would have any memory of it as she grew up.

On the other side of the aisle sat his sister-in-law Beth, and her husband of a year Caspian. James was pleased they had somehow managed to get their schedules to align in order to take these ten days away together in Greece; he knew how much Lee missed spending time with her sister, in the year that she had been living in Scotland. When the two had married, Beth had moved in with Caspian in Edinburgh as that was where his job was, but James had always thought they would move back to Devon... they had both seemed so happy there.

As the time passed, he wondered if he had been wrong.

"How's work?" Caspian asked him across the aisle. They had boarded early as they were with a child, and so instead of waiting in the departure lounge, they were sat on the plane as it slowly filled.

"Same old," James said with a grin. "But I'm in line for a promotion, which would be a lot more responsibility..."

"That's great!" Caspian said, shifting in his seat. His tall frame seemed far too large for the space he had, but he wasn't one to complain.

"How about you? Things still going well in Edinburgh?" He heard about Beth and Caspian's life through Lee on a semi-regular basis, but it had been a while since he had chatted directly with Caspian. He'd forgotten how much he liked him; it was nice to talk to someone who seemed so genuine.

"Busy," Caspian said, and James had the feeling he was choosing his words carefully. "Beth's writing's taking off, of course-"

Beth rolled her eyes and elbowed him, but she was grinning.

"We've got all three books on our bookshelf!" James said. "Signed, and pride of place!"

Beth blushed, and Caspian laughed. "They're on our mantlepiece! And work's busy... a lot of responsibility. I'm managing more people now."

"How's that?"

Caspian shrugged. "I feel like I get less and less time to actually work on publicity campaigns, and more time just organising people. But I guess that's just how it goes, when you move up the ladder."

"I guess," James said.

"Good afternoon, this is your Captain speaking." James settled down into his seat as the captain talked about cruising altitudes and arrival times, and let his mind wander as the safety information was run through by the flight attendants.

There was more than one worry on his mind. Earlier in the year, his dad had been diagnosed with cancer. It wasn't advanced, thank goodness, and he had started treatment - but they were a close-knit family, and James found his mind wandering to how his dad was doing frequently. In fact, he had debated whether he should even be going away, but his whole family - mother, brother and sister, as well as his dad - had all insisted that he should. That nothing was going to happen in the ten days he was in Greece. And he felt like he needed this break; that Lee needed this break.

But it didn't stop him worrying.

He glanced at Lee who flashed him a smile before turning back to Holly. She was busy trying to distract her, both so that she did not get overexcited too quickly and so that she didn't get scared when they eventually did take off. Although neither Lee nor James were scared of flying, they had no idea how the little girl would cope with it.

On the other side of the aisle, more distraction was taking place - although that was because Beth <u>was</u> afraid of flying. She'd confessed to him when they'd arrived at the airport, that she had considered having several drinks to get through it, but she had decided to limit her drinking back when she and Caspian were doing long-distance and it had got a bit too regular, and now she didn't want to start drinking again to deal with her fears.

Instead she talked, and read, and gripped Caspian's hand far too tightly as the plane doors closed and they finally began to move.

James watched Holly as she leaned against Lee, looking out the window with nothing but excitement on her little face. It made his heart feel warm, and he put an arm awkwardly around both of them as they accelerated and lifted up, up, into the air, seeing the houses and cars become smaller and smaller until it looked like a little toy town beneath them. Holly gasped and pointed and laughed, and then they were above the clouds, the sky clear and blue and the plane seeming to float on the sea of white fluff.

"Well that went surprisingly well," James said, as Holly settled back in her seat with a film on an iPad and a pair of over-ear headphones that looked comically large on her.

"She's always pretty laid back!" Lee said with a smile, but James thought she looked relieved. "I'm so ready to lie by a pool while you play with her endlessly in the water..."

James laughed, knowing he was more than happy for that to be the case. They had rented a self-catered villa, with its own pool and only a short walk to the beach. It seemed a pretty ideal location for the five of them to enjoy some sunshine, some drinks and hopefully let go of the stresses of their everyday lives.

Although the flight was less than four hours, by halfway through the three females were all fast asleep. Lee leant against the window of the plane, with Holly scrunched up against her, and Beth's head had fallen onto Caspian's shoulder.

James looked up from his book when he heard a loud snore, although he wasn't quite sure which of the three it had come from. He caught Caspian's eye and they both stifled a laugh.

"Good book?" Caspian asked, nodding his head at the thriller in James's hand.

"Not bad. I don't get much time to read, normally, so I thought I'd make the effort while we're away!"

"I know the feeling," Caspian said. "Although I've read Beth's books!"

"Of course," James said with a smile. "I did manage to fit those ones in!"

"How's your dad?" Caspian asked. "Beth said he wasn't very well..."

James sighed. "It's cancer," he said, never sure how much was shared through the pipeline of information between the two sisters. "Not terminal, thank god, although the word itself is scary enough."

"It definitely is," Caspian said, concern in his warm brown eyes.

"It's hard..." James said, trying to find the words to express what he was feeling. He kept his voice low, both to stop the others from waking and because they weren't feelings he wanted to share publicly. "He's just always been there, you know? And I guess the dreaded C-word - even if it's treatable, which they seem to think it is, makes you think about mortality. I mean, he won't be round for ever..."

"None of us will," Caspian said with a shrug. "I mean - I didn't mean that quite as harshly as it sounded. None of us know when our time might be up... I think we have to just make the most of every opportunity we have. Although that's not always so easy to do."

"No, you're right," James said, letting his legs spill out into the aisle for a moment as cramp threatened to become an issue. "It's easy to let work take over, isn't it."

"Tell me about it," Caspian said with a roll of his eyes. "This holiday is a good enforced break! Anyway, if you need to talk, you know where I am - I lost my dad a long time ago, but I think I still understand what you're saying."

"Thanks, Cas," he said, and as they lapsed into silence again he pondered those words. He had forgotten, if truth be told, that Caspian has lost his father as a child. He looked to Holly, and felt a pull in his heart; that would be so tough. Tough to think about not being there as Holly grew up, and tough to think about Holly not having a father around from such a young age.

And yet he didn't find it much easier to think about not having a father around himself.

As the seatbelt sign was turned back on for landing, he tried to move his thoughts away from the morbid direction they were headed in. Caspian was right; he needed to enjoy the moments. Because who knew how many of them anyone had left?

CHAPTER THREE
Beth

Beth drifted in and out of sleep while the plane flew through the air, finding it easier to stay calm if she zoned out than if people were constantly asking her if she was okay. Her head rested comfortably against Caspian's shoulder, and she kept her fingers entwined with his, feeling comforted in the fact that he was close.

She'd been afraid of planes for just over a year - a relatively short period of time for a phobia, she knew, but it was one she really wished she could overcome. Back when they'd been in a long distance relationship, she'd hopped on a plane pretty regularly to travel the many, many miles between Devon and Scotland. It hadn't really fazed her; it was quicker, and somehow cheaper, than the train, and her time with Caspian was limited enough.

And then one journey, before they got married, had changed everything. There had been heavy wind and rain forecast, but the plane was still running and Beth was more worried about being delayed than she had been about the weather impacting her flight. She'd got to the airport with extra time to spare, for what was going to be her last visit before she moved properly to Scotland. She had been living there most of the time for the last few months, but they had decided to sign a new lease together once they were married, and so she was still splitting her time - although it was definitely skewed towards Edinburgh.

Amazingly, they'd boarded on time, and take off had been a breeze - and then the turbulence had hit. Over and over again, with the seatbelt sign never being turned off - and still she hadn't panicked. Not until she'd seen the flight attendant look freaked out. That, and the semi-emergency landing they'd had to make into Edinburgh airport, had been enough to put Beth off flying for life.

And yet somehow here she was - and although she knew in her mind that it was a calm day and the journey was smooth, it was taking a lot of self-control to stop herself freaking out.

She heard bits of James's conversation, and felt desperately sad for them both. She knew how much losing his father had affected Caspian; and she knew how close James was to his dad. Contemplating death was not an easy thing; she didn't even like to think about anything happening to her father. It wasn't that they were as close as James and his dad, but Ted Davis had only come back into their lives in the last couple of years after a decades-long absence, and Beth felt they had a lot of lost time to catch up on.

She drifted back off to sleep and tried not to dwell on that conversation again.

*   *   *

Feeling a little stiff and achy, but relieved that the plane had touched down without a hiccup, Beth followed Caspian down the steps and towards the arrivals gate. They held hands and grinned as the Grecian heat hit them like a wall after the air-conditioned plane, and when the Knights caught up with them, they were smiling too.

"Don't get heat like that back in Scotland," Caspian said.

"Do you get any heat in Edinburgh?" Lee asked as they followed everyone else towards the baggage reclaim belts.

"Oh, you're so hilarious, *Shirley*," Beth said with a giggle, feeling fairly protective of her new home.

They waited for what seemed like an age for their suitcases to appear, along with many other irritated looking families. They were all keen to get out and enjoy the beautiful weather - but alas, their luggage had other plans.

First came Holly's luggage, a ride-along unicorn suitcase that was exceptionally easy to spot and came with the first round of luggage. Then James and Caspian's suitcases, both navy, with tags around them that made them easy to identify among the sea of similar cases in the next round of luggage.

And then they waited.

The same grey suitcase with a broken zip and a sparkly star on the front went round and round the belt, with no-one claiming it, but nothing else came. Only two families were left waiting now, aside from them, and they all looked equally fed up.

Holly had started to cry, and James had given in and handed her back the iPad.

Beth was regretting not eating lunch. The flying nerves had made her think it wasn't a great idea, but now dinner time was fast approaching and she was starving.

"It would be ours, wouldn't it," Lee said with a groan. "When do you think we go and say something?"

They all glanced at the board above the belt. It did still say their flight...they all hoped it would not be long until the sisters' cases appeared.

"There, there!" Beth said, pointing to the black case that was coming through the hole in the wall. "That looks like mine!"

She dashed over, pleased to see her rainbow-coloured strap - until she realised it was hanging off, and the contents of her suitcase were spilling out for all to see.

"What the-"

She dragged it off before it got away from her again, trying not to let any of her underwear fall out - but there was no way of knowing what might've fallen out before it had reached her.

"Brilliant."

"Oh no, Beth," Lee said, looking anxiously around her sister for her own case. "What's happened to it!"

"Either they think I'm suspicious and have torn through it, or they aren't as careful with them as we'd like to think. I just hope nothing has gone missing..."

"We'll go and complain," Caspian said. "It's ridiculous that it has come out in that state."

"Is mine ever going to even appear?" Lee asked, glancing at Holly, who was slumped against James's suitcase, looking like she might fall asleep - not the best start to their relaxing getaway.

"There's a few more coming," James said, and when Lee's case appeared, looking rather dented but at least still closed, they all breathed a sigh of relief.

"It can only get better!" James said as they walked towards the exit - and Beth sincerely hoped so.

*   *   *

After nearly an hour trying to find out who to complain to about their damaged luggage, and then a twenty minute drive in their hire car - that Beth was relieved she was not having to drive - they finally arrived at their villa.

The evening sun hit the exposed stone walls, sparkling off the pool and reminding them why they had decided to come away. All were tired and all were hungry, but they took a moment to look at the beautiful house they would get to call home for almost a fortnight, before Holly reminded them just how hungry she was in a very loud shout.

Thankfully they had stopped at a shop for some basics, and so while they figured out which room was which (it was pretty obvious - the one with the child sized bed in a small side-room was Lee and James's), James cooked a quick pasta dish that all of them claimed was the best thing they had ever eaten.

The warm evening air made it perfect to sit out on the veranda, and once they had finished eating and Lee had put an exhausted Holly to bed, they sat with a glass of wine each and watched the sun set. Beth was pleased she felt confident enough to have a glass of wine when she was with people; she didn't seem to lose control then. But she would have hated to miss out on that feeling of sharing a bottle with her family as they quietly contemplated the view.

"What a day," Beth said with a sigh.

"All's well that ends well," Caspian said, and Beth nodded.

"Even if the security staff have probably seen all my underwear."

They laughed together, and Beth shook her head as James offered to refill her glass. One was plenty.

"I've missed spending time with you," Lee said, giving her sister's hand a squeeze.

"Me too," said Beth. "I love Edinburgh - but it's far!"

"And I'm always so busy with Holly, and the cafe, and the law work... I know I don't come and see you enough."

She had been once, but Beth truly didn't blame her. "Hey, you're pretty much superwoman as it is. I know it's tough."

"Maybe you'll be busy with your own little one soon!" Lee said as she finished a second glass of wine.

Beth shrugged, and smiled. "I don't think so."

"I bet you'll get broody-"

"I'm busy with my writing."

"But you-"

"Lee, drop it." Beth knew her tone was sharp, but she was getting a bit sick of people assuming she would be pregnant any day, just because she and Caspian had been married a year. They were perfectly happy as just the two of them for now - maybe forever - so why couldn't everyone else be?

There was silence for a moment; neither of the two men seemed to want to get in between the sisters, and it seemed Lee didn't know what to say.

"Sorry, Beth, I just meant-"

"It's fine. Can we just drop it? Please?"

Lee nodded, and Caspian swooped in with a question about the cafe, letting Beth fade from the conversation for a few minutes.

She felt him squeeze her hand and knew, without words, that he understood her frustration. Even if she wasn't totally sure she understood it herself.

CHAPTER FOUR
Caspian

After a slightly awkward end to the evening, they all turned in early, wanting to make the most of a full day of beautiful weather the following morning. Their room was a comfortable temperature, thanks to the air conditioning. The crisp white sheets were pulled tight on the king size bed, and while Beth got ready in the ensuite, Caspian pulled back the covers and then wandered to the balcony that had views out to the sea.

He was looking forward to swimming in that ocean tomorrow. While he had previously swum almost every night in the sea when he lived in Devon, in Scotland that was a little less practical - and when they were in Devon now, it was to visit his mum or Lee, and they didn't have much spare time.

Caspian turned as he heard Beth re-enter the room, dressed in a light nightdress that he didn't think he'd seen before. The look on her face, though, made his heart ache, and he knew that she wasn't completely over the events of the evening.

She climbed into bed and he got ready quickly, slipping beneath the sheets wearing nothing, as he normally did when the weather was warm.

"Are you okay?" he asked. Her blonde hair was fanned out on the pillow and her eyes met his for a few moments before she spoke.

"It just seems that all anyone thinks we should be doing is having a baby. You don't know the number of people who keep going on about it, especially as we've been married a year."

"I didn't realise people had been going on about it so much," he said, wrapping an arm around her waist and pulling her close.

"I know we said we weren't thinking about it yet," Beth said, "But I'm worried, with all these people banging on about it..."

"Beth," he said, pressing his lips to her forehead. "It's completely our decision. And you know I'm not desperate about having kids right now."

"What if..." Beth sighed, and then spoke the words that had clearly been bothering her.

"What if I never want to? My mum, your mum, Lee, the women in my writing group - they all go on about it being some inevitability. But I like our life - I like the freedom to be able to go where we want, to spend Sunday in bed if we want to, that I can write whenever." She wriggled closer to him, until her head rested on his chest and she could feel the steadying rise and fall beneath her ear. "I like it being just me and you. What if that doesn't change?"

"Then we re-evaluate and see how we both feel, and take it from there. It's a bridge we don't need to cross right now - and if we never do, we never do." He hooked a finger under her chin and lifted her head from his chest so he could see her face.

"I love *you*, Beth, and we can decide everything else as we go on." He smiled; "We've got the rest of our lives together."

She smiled then, unable to resist the pull of his words, and then let her lips brush against his before settling her head back on his chest.

"I shouldn't have snapped at Lee," she said.

"No, probably not. But talk to her - I'm sure she'll understand."

Beth bit her lip; "I think they're struggling to have a second. She's not said it outright, but a couple of comments she's made..." She sighed again, feeling a wave of tiredness hit her as she stifled a yawn. "It's never simple is it."

"No," he said, letting his eyes drift closed as he held his wife in his arms. "Nothing worth it ever is though."

*   *   *

Light streamed through the curtains that Beth and Caspian had forgotten to close, and when Caspian opened his eyes he didn't realise quite how early it was. Beth slept more peacefully now, although she rolled over and hid her head beneath the duvet when Caspian moved and the sunlight hit her face. He stifled a laugh, and then slipped from the sheets. He glanced over at his phone and realised it wasn't even six am. Considering getting back into bed for a second, he instead grabbed his swimming trunks and a towel, and quickly threw on a t-shirt and shorts.

The sea was calling, and he was pretty sure he would be back before anyone else was even awake.

They could see the sea from their balcony, and so he knew roughly where he was going. He hadn't bothered to bring headphones, just his phone in his pocket in case he got lost or anyone worried about where he was, and as soon as he got outside he began to jog in the direction of the sea. He felt his muscles waking up, the burn that he had learned to enjoy as he increased his speed and felt himself get slightly out of breath. Once he had hated running; now, exercise was such an essential part of him that he couldn't imagine going days without feeling this adrenaline rush like he once had.

The roads were almost deserted, and he took in the sights and sounds of the Grecian countryside, letting his mind wander as his body moved.

Did he want children?

In the abstract, he thought he probably did, although he had to admit it wasn't something he thought about regularly. He was married, and in his thirties - all reasons people would have for thinking he and Beth might be having children soon.

But he also knew he was quite happy just the two of them. He liked the freedom; he still craved every minute of her company. The year they had spent married and living together had certainly not dulled that. So no, it wasn't something that he wanted right now - but ever?

If she never wanted to have children, could he cope with that?

As he reached the ocean, he took a deep breath and felt the saltiness in his throat.

Yes, he could. He loved her, and that was enough.

No-one knew what the future held, anyway.

He waited until he was a couple of metres away from the millpond-still water to remove his trainers, socks and t-shirt. His shorts were worn over his trunks, for speed, and so it did not take long until he was ready to get in the water. Hiding his phone underneath his clothes, he took long strides towards to water, wading out until it was deep enough to begin to swim.

The air around him was already balmy, despite the early hour, and the water felt a pleasant temperature. His whole body felt hot and sweaty from the run, anyway, and as he began to swim through the water, he felt it wash away the grime from the exercise, as well as the tension in his muscles. He forgot how freeing it was to just swim in the open water, especially this early where there was no-one really around. There was something special about swimming like this - different to being constrained in a pool, which he did sometimes resort to. As he moved through the water, letting it soak through his hair as he dipped his head to take carefully timed breaths, he found all thoughts disappearing and his focus turning solely to the power of his body in the water.

As the sun grew higher in the sky, his arms eventually grew weary, and he exited the water to a slightly busier beach - although luckily, no-one had gone near his clothes or phone. Checking the time, he knew he should probably be heading home - the run would take a little time, and he didn't want Beth worrying about where he had gone. She hadn't rung, though, and he smiled as he pictured her still in bed, peacefully unaware of the sunshine streaming through the window and heating up the world outside.

After a quick towel dry, he threw his clothes back on and started back on the road, feeling totally peaceful and very much ready for some breakfast.

*   *   *

When he arrived back at the villa, Lee, James and Holly were sat at the breakfast table, and the most amazing smell of bacon and eggs was wafting through the air.

"I thought you were still asleep!" Lee said, smiling as she handed Holly some orange juice.

"I presume Beth still is," he said. "I just wanted a swim!"

"I didn't even hear the car!"

"I ran," Caspian said with a shrug.

"Wow. That's dedication. Breakfast?" James asked, shaking the frying pan a little.

"Sounds amazing. Can I just jump in the shower? I'll be ten minutes - I can heat it back up."

James took a seat next to his wife. "No worries - I was planning to make some more when you and Beth came down anyway."

He took the stairs two at a time, feeling grateful once again for Beth pushing him to figure out how to take the time off so they could come away. He felt less stressed already, and it had only been hours since they had arrived.

When he entered the bedroom, Beth was taking up most of the bed, her eyes slightly open and her hair spread across both pillows.

"Morning," he said. "I hope I didn't wake you."

She shook her head, propping herself up on her elbows. "You didn't. What time is it?"

"Coming up to eight. James is making breakfast!"

"I thought I could smell something good," she said with a smile. "Have you eaten?"

"Been for a run - and a swim!"

Beth laughed and rolled her eyes. "I should have guessed."

He pulled his t-shirt over his head and dropped it onto the floor, leaning over to carefully kiss Beth without touching the bed before he'd washed.

"Let me jump in the shower," he said. "And I'll meet you downstairs. The kettle sounded like it was on!"

"Perfect," Beth said.

Caspian didn't bother to lock the door as he stripped off and stepped into the shower. It was nice and powerful, and the water cascaded over his head, washing off the mix of salt water and sweat from his morning's exercise.

The shower door slid open and he grinned through the water as Beth stood there, in that little pink nightie, a cheeky smile on her face.

"Mind if I join you?" she asked, her clothing dropping to the floor, and he stepped to one side.

"Never, Mrs Blackwell," he said, closing the door to keep the heat and the water in, and the rest of the world out...

CHAPTER FIVE
Lee

Eventually, Beth and Caspian appeared at the breakfast table, and Lee clicked the kettle on as they took their seats. She'd finished her breakfast, and Holly was wearing the evidence of hers across her face, but James had another set of bacon and eggs on the go and Lee was desperate for another coffee.

"Morning!" she said, smiling at her sister and hoping the awkwardness from the previous night had dissipated. They rarely fell out, and she certainly hadn't meant to offend her. She hadn't thought the joke would be that much of an issue - but perhaps, with the distance between them, they just hadn't been sharing so much lately. She knew she hadn't shared much about their difficulties conceiving with her little sister; it was all so much easier when they were face to face than the phone conversations they had these days.

"Morning!" Beth's smile seemed genuine, and Lee relaxed. They would have a nice day in the sunshine, and everything would be like it was before.

"I cannot believe Caspian had already been out exercising before the rest of us even got dressed!" she said, and saw Beth blush; she wasn't too sure why, but decided it probably wasn't appropriate to ask.

"So," James said, dishing up Beth and Caspian's breakfast. "What shall we do today?"

"Lie by the pool?" Beth suggested. "The sun looks amazing out there."

"We could go into town this afternoon," Lee suggested. "Get some food, look at the market..."

*   *   *

Having a private pool was ideal; no racing out to make sure they could get sun loungers or having to deal with loud people splashing around. Although, Lee thought as she and Beth spread out their towels on loungers next to each other, perhaps they would be classed as the loud, splashy ones. They had only been outside for five minutes and already James was in the water, trying to coax Holly in.

"What a beautiful day," Beth said, putting her over-sized sunglasses on and lying down.

"Gorgeous," Lee agreed, a little distracted as she watched Holly. She was sun-creamed to within an inch of her life and wore a float-filled swim suit, but it still made Lee nervous to watch her so near the water.

"Don't let her fall in!" she warned James. She knew James would be watching her like a hawk; he was an amazing father, and his attention never wandered from his little daughter. Still, her anxiety never totally disappeared.

"I've got her!" James said putting out his hands for Holly to take hold of. Eventually she did, and he lifted her into the shallow end of the water where she squealed and splashed happily.

Lee sighed, and then put her sunglasses back on. She had to step back and let James do his thing... it had always been an issue for her. Perhaps that was how she was somehow running a cafe, a one-woman law firm and trying to do as much of the parenting as was physically possible. She couldn't remember the last time she got a full night's sleep - and it wasn't all down to Holly. No, she stayed up too late working, got up too early to get things organised and woke herself up worrying about things that needed to get done far more often than Holly woke her up.

Holly, she was fairly sure, had inherited her father's laid-back attitude to life, and so it was just Lee up worrying in the middle of the night.

"So," Beth said, watching as Caspian and James crouched in the shallow end to keep their shoulders under, sending Holly floating between them. Her giggles filled the air, and Lee felt her heart melt at the sight of the two men so focussed on just making her smile. "About last night. I'm sorry I snapped at you."

Lee's attention turned more fully to her sister. "I'm sorry if I upset you!" Lee said. "I really didn't mean to."

"I know. It's something that's been getting to me for a while, and you just happened to say it at the wrong time, that's all. I shouldn't have snapped."

"It's fine."

"It's just... I'm sick of people assuming I'm going to get pregnant at any moment. I'm happy as I am, and I may be happy like this forever - and I don't want to have to justify that to anyone else."

Lee paused for a moment, making sure she wasn't going to say anything that would offend. "That's totally fair. I was wrong to assume. It's just..." She looked back to where James was holding Holly on her back in the water, encouraging her to kick her legs. "I'm so desperate for another. It's all I think about some days... and I know I'm lucky to have what I have, but I just didn't think it would be this hard to get pregnant again."

She laughed, although it sounded like it was dangerously close to a sob. "It was so easy last time. Too easy! And now we've been trying for nearly a year and nothing..."

Beth moved towards Lee with a scraping noise as her lounger shifted on the flagstones. She took hold of Lee's hand and gave it a tight squeeze; "I didn't realise you'd been trying so long," she said. "Oh Lee."

"I have so many things going on - I shouldn't even have time for another baby! But I'm not twenty-five any more... maybe it's just too late."

Beth shook her head. "You're not that old, Lee. And like you said, you got pregnant with Holly so easily! Have you been to the doctors?"

Lee sniffed and shook her head. "Not yet. Seems a bit too real."

"You'd tell me not to put my head in the sand," she told her big sister. "Seeing a doctor won't make anything worse, will it - and maybe there's some easy fix."

"Or maybe I need to accept that I have one amazing daughter, and stop trying to be greedy for more."

"Oh Lee," Beth said. "You're not being greedy. Maybe you're just doing too much - with everything you do in a day I don't know where you get time to sleep, let alone do anything else!"

There was a suggestive tone to her sister's voice that made Lee laugh, despite the sadness she was feeling.

"You're probably right. And I know I need to see a doctor... before it really is too late."

Beth leaned back on her own seat, and glanced over at Caspian, who was now doing some speedy lengths through the water in a perfect-looking front crawl.

"The way you talk, you'd think you were approaching sixty!"

"Feels like it some days," Lee said, closing her eyes against the powerful heat of the sun.

"Try to relax on this holiday, hey? You never know, it might do you some good!"

"Yes, wise one," Lee said, and they both giggled.

It was good they'd talked, Lee thought as they quietly sunned themselves for a while. She understood Beth's anger a little more, even if Lee felt so differently about the topic than she did. And Beth was right; *not* calling the doctor certainly didn't solve the problem.

Her eyes had been shut for ten minutes or so when she felt icy cold hands on her stomach and she shrieked loudly enough to make Beth half-topple off her lounger.

"Holly!" she screamed as cold water dripped off her daughter's hands onto her warm, bare skin, and then burst out laughing. "I was not expecting that, monkey!"

And then they were all laughing, and Caspian was persuading Beth to give him a hug despite the fact that he was cold and dripping water too, and Lee felt her heart return to a place of peace. Yes, there was more she wanted, but she didn't want to forget just how much she already had.

CHAPTER SIX
James

"You look great in that bikini," James murmured to Lee as they fetched drinks from the kitchen for everyone. Lee put down the jug of water she was carrying and glanced down at her black bikini. She had ummed and ahhed about whether to wear it; since having Holly, she'd not been so keen to wear anything that showed the stretch marks on her stomach, but since it was just family, and it had been almost three years in which those angry red marks had faded to silver stripes, she had decided to go for it.

"Really?"

James's eyes met hers and he placed one hand lightly on her waist. He felt her skin tingle beneath his fingertips, and it felt warm where his fingers were still cool from his time in the water.

"Really," he said. "You're always beautiful..."

Lee smiled and rested her hand against the side of his face. There was a trace of stubble beneath her fingertips, where he had decided to not bother shaving that morning, and he could feel her breath against his skin as she breathed in and out close to his face.

"And you look very nice without a shirt on," she said.

"Ah, next to Caspian, I'm not so sure I'm anything to look at."

"Are you fishing for compliments, James Knight?" Lee asked with a cheeky grin on her face. "You are the sexiest man out there - and you are all mine." She pressed her lips to his then and he wrapped his arms around her waist tighter, feeling the spontaneity that had been there when they were first together, but that had not been so present in recent months when a child and several jobs took up so much of their time.

"All yours," he said with a smile, and then he kissed her again, less gently this time, and he could feel her hands on his bare back, until-

"Do you need any-oh. Sorry." A giggle, and then Beth had disappeared from the room, clearly amused by walking in on her sister and husband kissing in the kitchen.

James sighed, and Lee rolled her eyes. "Sisters, eh," she said, and James grabbed the cans of beer while Lee took the water jug.

"There's always tonight," James said, and Lee felt a shiver of promise flutter through her as they re-joined their family.

CHAPTER SEVEN
Beth

The afternoon had been filled with an enjoyable stroll around the local market, and while none of them spoke any Greek, the market sellers had enough English between them to do a good job at selling their wares.

At a stall selling fresh seafood, Caspian became very interested and Beth left him to it as he decided to purchase food for that evening's meal. Lee and James were dragged to stalls selling toys and anything that sparkled by their magpie of a daughter, and Beth made her own way over to a young man with an impressive array of notebooks on his table. She had always been a bit of a stationary fiend, and every time she had a new idea for a story she bought a new notebook -

although sometimes it happened the other way round. In fact, she now had a whole shelf of notebooks in their Edinburgh home - and not all of them were filled!

Somehow, her writing was earning enough to make her feel that doing it full time was an option. It wasn't loads - she wasn't going to be a millionaire anytime soon - but as she'd worked minimum wage jobs all her life, she was happy with anything that brought some money in. Now she and Caspian were married, she didn't feel so bad about him earning so much more than she did - although she hoped it would not be that way forever. She was exploring other publishing options - including possibly self-publishing - in the hopes that writing could be the thing that would support her until she wanted to retire. That was an awfully long way off, and the small income it brought in at the minute didn't leave a lot of room for holidays or treats - but it was the dream she was aiming for.

She couldn't resist, therefore, when she saw all the different notebooks, which he told her proudly in broken English were handmade. They were beautiful; mainly bound in leather, with thick cream pages that were just begging for words. Even though she was writing more and more with each passing month, she still felt the need to write longhand before typing it - and so another notebook felt like the perfect treat to buy herself from the market.

Relieved that the seller wasn't too pushy, she spent several minutes browsing, picking and changing her mind before going back to the original. Then, hidden at the back behind several others, she spotted a dark-brown leather journal, with a cord wrapped around it to keep it closed. An intricate tree of life was embossed on the front, and she knew that one was the one.

As he packaged it up and took her money, she felt a hand on her waist and looked up to see Caspian, laden with two bags which, from the smell, included a decent amount of seafood.

"I've got a great idea for dinner!" he said excitedly, and they walked away from the stall hand-in-hand, Beth finding her mind wandering to ideas to fill that notebook, as often seemed to happen when she had chosen a new one.

*   *   *

After an early dinner, Holly went to bed exhausted from swimming, walking and having far too much excitement to have a nap earlier in the day. Lee brought the monitor down and the adults sat out on the veranda, sharing a pitcher of sangria and laughing about Caspian's enthusiasm for the meal he was cooking them.

"Although," Lee said, between sips of the sweet sangria, "If I don't have to cook, I'm more than happy."

"When do we ever cook!" Beth said with a laugh, and their husbands rolled their eyes and smiled. It was true -

neither of the Davis sisters had been gifted with skills in the kitchen.

Caspian disappeared to tweak and taste whatever he was surprising them with, and their conversation turned to Edinburgh.

"Are you happy, there?" Lee asked, as she leant back in her chair and stretched her legs so her feet touched James's beneath the table. "It seemed amazing, when we came up."

"The city is wonderful," Beth said, sipping her drink slowly so it would last. "I get so much inspiration to write there, and finding writing groups and interesting places to write so easily is great."

"But..."

Beth laughed; her sister knew her well. "You know. I miss Devon; I miss you lot. It's a long way from everyone we know."

"Will you be there for the long term, do you think?" James asked, and Beth took a moment to answer. It was something she tried not to think about regularly; she was happy in Edinburgh, and so there seemed no use in dwelling on where she might rather be.

"We'll see if things change with Caspian's job, I guess," she said. "I know he misses his mum, and the countryside... but his career is doing so well, and it's not exactly a hardship to live in Edinburgh!"

It was then, to quiet applause from the rest of the family, that Caspian brought out the dish he had been working on all evening.

"Greek paella!" he announced, placing the steaming hot frying pan in the middle of the table. "I was going to make the Spanish version I've made before, but the seller at that seafood stall gave me this recipe, and I couldn't resist."

"Smells fantastic," James said, reaching over to dish some out onto his plate.

"Thanks Caspian," Lee said with a smile, scooching her chair forward so she could reach the table.

They dug in, going silent for a few minutes as they enjoyed the good food and watched the setting sun over the sea in the distance.

"Beach tomorrow?" Beth suggested, and they all nodded.

"Although Caspian will probably be there before we're awake again!" Lee said, glancing in the distance. "It looks like a hell of a long way to run, especially with everything we'll need for a day at the beach!"

Caspian smirked; "We can take the car tomorrow!"

"Too right we can!"

As the balmy air began to cool a little, and plates were scraped clean, James raised his glass with a smile. "If it's okay - and not too old-fashioned - I'd like to make a toast. My dad always does at big family occasions, and I feel this qualifies as one." He smiled at them, but Beth was sure she could see sadness in his eyes that he was not voicing. "To family, to friendship, to love."

They raised their glasses and as the sun set on their gathering, Beth felt very grateful for a sister and a brother-in-law that she was so happy to spend time with; family that she knew would show up, no matter the situation. Wasn't that what everyone wanted?

CHAPTER EIGHT
Caspian

With a large array of towels, beach toys and food spread around them, the Knights and the Blackwells took up a decent chunk of the beach, which - thanks to the lovely weather - just got busier as the day went on. The sand was soft beneath their feet and the calm water seemed to go on forever into the distance, gently lapping at the shore. Beth and Lee lay on a towel each, propped up on their elbows, quietly chatting while Holly snoozed between them under the shade of a large umbrella.

A few metres away, Caspian and James were very happily finding their inner children. With Holly, they had built an impressive sandcastle, and now that she was asleep they had added a moat and a tunnel to the water, and were excitedly waiting for the sea to fill it. The calm water was not so helpful for that endeavour, and so there was plenty of time to stand around chatting, just out of hearing reach of their wives.

"How's your mum doing, without you living nearby?" James asked, shielding his eyes from the sun and considering asking Lee to throw him his sunglasses. "Lee said you're pretty close!"

Caspian shrugged; "She misses me being close, I think, but she's doing all right. To be honest, I'm pretty sure she's seeing someone!"

"Wow! Is that a new thing?"

"From what I've gathered - although for a while, I'll admit I tried to ignore it was happening - I think they started going out for the odd meal a year ago and it's just gone on from there. He was my old piano teacher, so I do vaguely know him..."

"Good for her!" James said with a grin. "Must be a bit weird for you though."

Caspian ran a hand through his dark hair. "Very. As far as I know - and I admit, I've never really asked - she's been single ever since dad died! I am glad though, that she won't be on her own all the time - when I don't think about it."

James smiled. "Do you think you might move back down?" he asked, and Caspian looked back up at where Lee and Beth were intently talking before formulating his answer.

"Between us - if that's okay - I'm ready to move back now. But Beth has really fallen for Edinburgh, and I asked her to move her whole life for me... I don't feel I can ask her to do it all again so soon."

James nodded; "I won't say anything. But have you talked to her? Maybe she feels the same?"

Caspian shook his head. "At the beginning, I think she would have jumped at the chance, but now... she's got her writing groups, and her series set in Edinburgh... but if I mention it, I think she might do it for me, and I want her to make choices for her..."

"That's fair enough. Can you move your job back though? Wasn't that the whole issue?"

A smile played on Caspian's lips. "I've got a bit of a dream - a dream to set up my own business. And I could do that wherever, really. So much more is online these days, anyway." He shrugged, and glanced out to sea for a moment. "But of course there's risk involved, and at the minute mine's the more stable income - although Beth's doing so well with her writing."

"I think she'd want you to follow your dreams, too," James said, hoping he wasn't overstepping.

Caspian smiled; "She would. But I don't want her to have to give anything up so I can do this. Not right now."

"The water's coming!" James suddenly cried, and their serious conversation was put aside as they watched their moat fill with water. Holly was unfortunately still asleep, but their excitement was not dampened - and it just meant they could do it all over again when she was awake!

*　　*　　*

After a delicious picnic that Lee had packed, followed by ice creams from a little hut at the top of the beach, Caspian and Beth left James, Lee and Holly to their sandcastle building and took a stroll along the hot sands.

"Are you having a good time?" Beth asked, her arm wrapped around his waist. He could feel the heat of her skin against his in their swimming costumes, and he smiled as she gave a little shiver when his fingers grazed the skin above her hip bone.

"I really am," he said, taking a couple of steps to the right so his feet were in the shallows of the sea. "I can't remember when I felt so relaxed!"

"Sun, sea, sand, sangria..."

"Sex..." Caspian added, and Beth giggled. He pulled on her hand to stop her walking any further, and for a moment just watched her as the sun glinted off her blonde locks.

"You look beautiful," he said, and Beth blushed and touched her fingertips to his lips.

"You look devastatingly handsome - as always!"

"Do you fancy a swim, wife?" he asked, a cheeky glint in his eye.

"Only with you," she said, and hand-in-hand they waded out into the calm waters, needing to go a fair distance until it was deep enough to dip their shoulders.

"No military-style swimming today?" Beth asked with a smile, letting her head drop back so it rested on the surface of the water. When she raised it, water flowed down her bank from her hair and the sun glowed behind her like a halo.

"I think I can take it a little easier today," he said, encircling her waist in his arms and pulling her close to him. They both ducked their shoulders under the water, although the air around them was certainly not cool, and the smile on Beth's lips was mirrored in Caspian's.

"I love the sea," she said, and she was close enough that he could feel her breath against his skin.

"Me too," he said, letting his fingertips brush along her bare arm, trailing along her stomach and resting on her hip. He was rewarded with her skin prickling beneath his touch, and he was pleased that even after a year of marriage, and two years together, there was still such a strong spark of chemistry between them.

"It's nice being away with Lee and James," Beth was saying, although Caspian had to admit he was a little distracted by her bare skin beneath his fingers, the feeling of the glassy water surrounding them both like a bubble away from everyone else... "But it's nice to spend time just me and you."

Caspian nodded as the words filtered through, and then he let his lips brush against the side of her neck, her collar bone, her shoulder - nothing too inappropriate for a busy beach, but then they were far enough away from the shore that they probably weren't too clear to the crowds anyway.

His lips moved to hers and, just like that very first time, as they kissed he felt the fireworks fizzing in his mind and it took a lot of effort to remember to be appropriate. He held her close and felt like, in that moment in the sea, all their worries were a million miles away. They were just a boy and a girl, forgetting about the world around them and giving in to temptation.

"You're a bad influence, Mr Blackwell," Beth said when they pulled apart, grins on their faces.

"Me? I think you were the one who corrupted me, if I remember rightly."

And with that he swam away, laughing into the distance as Beth swam in a vain attempt to keep up with him.

CHAPTER NINE
Lee

"Go!" Lee shouted, shoving James playfully out of the door as Holly giggled. "I told you we are cooking tonight - so go out and talk with Caspian, or play with Holly - but stay out of the kitchen!"

"Fine, fine - just don't set anything on fire!"

"Cheeky," Beth said, and James picked up a squealing Holly and tossed her over his shoulder, heading out to the pool where Lee had heard the splashing sounds of Caspian swimming.

"Does Caspian exercise every day?" Lee asked Beth, looking at the array of ingredients on the counter and slightly regretting telling the boys they would cook.

"Pretty much," Beth said, grabbing a can of coke from the fridge. "Sometimes I feel guilty about watching him go for a run... then I usually open a bar of chocolate."

Lee laughed loudly enough that she saw James turn backwards to see what was up, before turning back to the pool and shouting something to Caspian that they couldn't hear.

"Do you know how to make a risotto?" she asked Beth.

"Yes, actually! James sent me a recipe and I've made it a few times for Caspian. That's why I suggested it!"

"Well, you're in charge then - I'll do as I'm told!"

"Yeah, right," Beth said with a snort, rolling up her sleeves and pulling out two chopping boards. "Here, you can do the onion."

"Hey, I can do as I'm told!" Lee said, a little offended by Beth's quick response.

"Lee, you're a born leader. You just like to be in charge - that's nothing to be ashamed of."

"Well..."

"And we both have to admit that cooking is a skill that does not come naturally to us."

Lee giggled at that, pouring herself a glass of wine and gesturing towards the bottle. Beth shook her head.

"That's fair enough." She began to chop while Beth started on the stock and the garlic, and for a few minutes they worked in silence, the sound of Caspian, James and Holly in the pool permeating the air. After a while, Lee asked, "How's the not-drinking thing going?" Some things, she found, were much easier to ask in person.

She worried a little in case the question would upset her sister, but instead Beth smiled. "Fine, actually. I don't drink alone - but there's never any reason to now, anyway. And I don't really ever get drunk, because I hate the feeling of being hungover. I seem to be able to cope with one glass of wine and can walk away after that."

"I'm really proud of you, Beth - it could have gone a very different way, and you turned it all around."

Beth shrugged and said no more, but blushed a little.

"Do you really think I can't follow instructions?" Lee asked, as the frying pan began to sizzle with the garlic and onion.

Beth rolled her eyes; "Can't let go, either, can you!" She laughed and poured the rice in before answering her sister. "It's not that you can't follow instructions, but that you can't take a back seat. I don't know how you ever get any sleep, with the amount of different things you're doing every day."

Lee sat down then, sipping on her glass of wine and watching her sister do the cooking - almost as if she were making a point.

"I guess I could be a bit less involved with some things..."

"Lee, you run two businesses, as well as raising a daughter and I presume spending some time with your husband! I'm not saying it's a bad thing... but if you're finding you're really stressed, and you know, things aren't going the way you planned.... Maybe you need to take a bit of a break from it all."

As they chatted, Beth slowly added the stock, checking regularly to make sure it wasn't burning. She was pleased she had one decent dish she could make - even if it got repeated fairly often!

"You're probably right," Lee said with a sigh. "But..." She took a moment, and a large sip of wine, before voicing the thoughts that had been in her head for a long while. "What if I give it all up, I relax, I go to the doctors... and I still don't get pregnant? Then what?"

Beth pulled out a dining room chair - which they had barely used, since they had taken almost all their meals out in the sunshine - and sat next to her sister. "Honestly? I think you appreciate the amazing daughter you have - no, wait, I'm not saying you don't already. I think if that bridge is the one you have to cross, then you will come to terms with it, you'll cross it and you'll get to a point where it'll feel right to only have the one. Or..."

"Or?"

"Or you'll consider other options. Adoption, surrogacy - no looking at me though."

They both laughed at that and Lee leant forward and gave her sister a tight hug. "Thanks, Beth. A lot of wisdom there..."

"Well, you know what they say about blondes." She grinned. "You're strong. If that's the bridge you come to, you'll cross it - but I still think it wouldn't hurt you to relax a bit."

"I've been saying that for months!" James said, walking in and catching the end of the conversation.

"Checking up on our cooking, are you?" Beth asked, stirring the risotto and feeling relieved she hadn't burnt it to the bottom while she had been distracted by the chatting.

"No, no, just getting a drink - Caspian is happily throwing Holly in the air, so no rush."

Lee laughed, but couldn't stop herself from taking a peek out of the large windows to make sure her daughter was okay. She was giggling happily as Caspian lifted her high into the air, let go for a second and then brought her gently crashing back into the water. Convinced she was safe, Lee turned back to her sister, and almost commented on what a good dad Caspian would be - before realising that was probably not the right thing to say.

James pressed a kiss to his wife's cheek, getting to the door before daring to comment - "Letting your sister do all the cooking are you?"

She threw a cushion at him, which he artfully ducked, before disappearing back out to the pool.

"Men," Lee said, rolling her eyes and standing to join Beth at the counter. "But I really should be helping you more..."

By the time dinner was served, Holly was exhausted and almost fell asleep with her face in the food twice. James offered to take her up and get her ready for bed, and as the three other adults lounged outside with full stomachs and tired limbs from swimming, walking and lying on the sand, they found themselves discussing flaws - more specifically, their own biggest flaws.

"Well, thanks to my sister," Lee said, raising her glass of wine towards Beth with a grin, "I can confidently say my biggest flaw is not being able to take a back seat!"

They laughed, and then Lee turned to her sister. "What about you?"

"Ooh, so many to choose from. A lack of organisational skills? Being too flighty?"

Lee snorted. "Once upon a time, maybe, but you've been married a year - not so flighty these days!"

"What about you, Caspian?" The wine was making her bold as she probed her brother-in-law. This was probably the longest they'd ever spent together, and she was pleased to find that they all got on despite the close proximity they were living in for these ten days.

"Hmmm," he said, taking a sip from his bottle of beer to give himself some thinking time. "Probably not communicating well enough!" he said.

James entered then, keen to join in, although when he discovered what they were sharing he was less enthusiastic.

"Too many to name, I'm sure!"

"I doubt that," Beth said with a grin. "Lee wouldn't put up with anyone who was less than practically perfect!"

"You've got very few faults," Lee agreed with a smile.

"Ooh, I'm messy!" Beth suddenly shouted. "Forgot to put that one in there."

Everyone laughed; "It was meant to be one fault!" Lee said, but Beth just grinned and shrugged.

"I guess I'm not great with confrontation," James finally said. "So I let people get away with far too much!"

The sun had been set for quite some time when they eventually all wandered off to bed. Lee was sure the wine had gone to her head; she felt warm all over and things were not quite in focus. As they entered the bedroom, she blasted up the air conditioning and lay down on the bed with a dramatic sigh.

James began to unbutton his shirt, his curly hair a little longer than he usually kept it, and he smiled at her slightly tipsy actions.

"Are you all right?" he asked with a chuckle.

Lee propped herself up on her elbows. "Do you think I walk all over you?"

"What?" His response was instantaneous. "No! Why on earth would you think that?"

He sat next to her on the bed, and she was distracted for a second by his shirtlessness, before remembering why she had been concerned.

"What you said at dinner... letting people get away with too much. Does that include me?"

James ran his fingers through Lee's hair, smoothing it away from her face. "Never, Lee. I can tell you anything."

Lee beamed at that; "I can tell you anything too."

"Good. That's the way it should be. No, I meant more with work - definitely not you."

Lee sighed and lay back on the bed, feeling like it was too much effort to keep propping herself up. "I'm sorry you feel that way," she said. "But very glad it's not me."

James lay down on the bed next to her, leaning on one arm so that he could see Lee's face.

"You make me feel like everything I have to say is important, Lee. Marrying you was the best thing I've ever done - aside from having Holly, of course."

Lee smiled, and then felt a tear rolling down her cheek.

"Hey, what did I say now?" James said, and although Lee was struggling herself with her alcohol-driven yo-yo emotions, she did know why she was suddenly upset.

"What if it's me? What if I can't carry another baby? Will you still love me then?"

He took her hand then, and she was a little shocked by the fierce emotion in his eyes and voice. "I will love you no matter what. And if we - and whatever the cause, it's always us, Lee - if we can't have another baby, I will still be overjoyed with our little family."

Lee felt more tears then, but they were tears of happiness - and she reached over to thread her fingers through his hair, pulling his head close to hers so she could kiss his lips. She felt a desperation to be close to him, close to this man she loved so much, close to this man who had changed the whole course of her life for the better.

"I love you," she murmured as she took a breath, and he whispered the words back, fervently responding to her kisses and reaching to pull her beach dress over her head.

Her worries melted into nothing for that night as she reminded herself how lucky she was to have a wonderful husband who she loved so very much.

CHAPTER TEN
James

When James woke the next morning, Lee was no longer in bed next to him and, after listening for a moment and hearing nothing in the adjoining room, he was fairly sure she and Holly had gone downstairs for breakfast.

He stretched out in the king-size bed, then wrapped the sheet tightly around himself. Thanks to Lee turning the air-conditioning to full, and the fact that he wasn't wearing any pyjamas, he was not particularly warm - in spite of the sunshine that was streaming through the windows.

After a quick shower - and a readjustment of the air con settings - James dressed and glanced at his phone, shocked he had slept in until almost ten. Shift work tended to throw off his sleeping pattern at home, but he was usually up and about by then; Lee must've disappeared quietly with Holly to let him sleep in, he thought with a smile.

A photo sent by Lee of Holly covered in yoghurt showed him they had indeed gone down for breakfast, and as he sent a smiley face in return he saw a text from his dad appear.

Hope you're having a lovely time! Keep the photos coming. Dad X

James stared at the words for a moment. He spoke to his dad regularly - saw him regularly, in fact - when they were at home - and yet since he had found out about his dad's illness, he'd felt somewhat separated from him. The worry that he would have to say goodbye - even though, of course, he knew logically that at some point it would happen - tore him up inside, and he felt himself pulling away even though that was the exact opposite of what he wanted to do.

He sat for a moment, hearing in the distance the chatter of his family downstairs, before hitting dial. He didn't even know what he wanted to say - just that he needed to hear his dad's voice in that moment.

"Hi, son!" His dad answered on the third ring. "Everything all right?"

"Yeah, all good here thanks - how about you?"

"Can't complain! The weather looks amazing - we've got rain, as usual!"

James laughed. "Holly's loving it - in the swimming pool every day!"

"We're loving the pictures," his dad said, and for a moment there was silence on the line. "Are you sure everything's okay, James?"

"I-" James realised he had no idea how to put what he was feeling into words. He had always been a fairly chatty lad, and had not struggled with sharing his emotions - but this was something completely alien to him. This fear that was lodged inside him... this inability to accept his dad was not invincible. "I've just been thinking a lot," he said, realising how little that really explained but not sure what to add.

"Always dangerous," Mark Knight said with a laugh, but there was concern there too. "About anything in particular?"

"About you... about you being ill. About something happening to you." He laughed to hide his discomfort in the topic, although he was sure his dad could see through it. "I'm struggling to not think about it, to be honest."

"Son," he said. "I'm fine."

"But dad-"

"Yes, I have cancer. Yes, it's bloody inconvenient. But - and I don't like to think of this either, but it's true - any one of us could be hit by a bus tomorrow. Cancer or no cancer, none of us know how long we've got left - and so there's no use getting hung up on thinking when time's going to run out. You've got to live it instead, James."

James was quiet for a moment as he digested his dad's words. There was wisdom there, for sure - but he wasn't convinced he could feel so calm about the whole situation.

"I love you, James, and I hate to see you struggling because of anything- especially because of me. All I want to do is live my life, my life that's filled with my wife, my kids, my amazing grandkids... do a bit of fishing, of course, and try to be happy. It doesn't work out like that every day, but that's the aim. I'm not going to spend any time fretting about the future - and neither should you."

"I love you too, dad," James said, and it was at that moment Lee came through the door.

'Are you okay?' she mouthed, and he nodded, but something in his eyes must have let her know he was not being completely honest. As he said goodbye to his dad and promised not to dwell on morbid thoughts any more, Lee wrapped her arms around him and held on tightly. She didn't ask anything of him, and for that he was grateful. For several moments they sat there, not speaking, James's head resting against hers as he tried to restore his positive outlook on the world.

When they heard a playful shriek downstairs, they both stood, and James smiled and pressed a kiss to his wife's cheek.

"Thank you."

"What for?"

"Just being here."

"Always."

"Talk later?"

She nodded, and inclined her head towards the door. "I'd better get down there before they let Holly have her weight in golden syrup..."

James laughed and let her go, before heading out onto the balcony for a moment to catch his breath. The sea in the distance was not as calm as the day before, and he could imagine the sound of it as it crashed onto the sand. Perhaps they would go there later, or visit the town, or lie by the pool and watch Holly throwing balls excitedly into the water.

Whatever they did, they would be making memories, and his dad's words stuck in his mind. That was what was important. After all, who knew how long anyone had left?

It was time to just live it.

CHAPTER ELEVEN
Beth

"Come on lovebirds!" Beth shouted up the stairs, before seeing her sister rounding the corner. "Oh, there you are! I've promised Holly we'll go to the park - sorry!"

Lee laughed. "You'd let her have her way with anything!" she said, re-entering the kitchen to find her daughter with only a little golden syrup in her hair.

"Going to the park!" Holly shouted, and Lee grinned.

"Apparently so! Come on then, let's get you dressed and see if daddy's ready. Shall we go out for lunch?"

"Sounds good to me," Caspian said. "There was a place by the beach that did amazing looking crab sandwiches!"

"You can take the boy out of Devon..." Lee said, and they all laughed as Lee took Holly upstairs for a quick wash-down before getting dressed.

"I swear half of parenting is just cleaning kids up," Beth said with a smile, pushing the newspaper away from Caspian's hands and perching on his lap. He wrapped his arms around her waist and buried his face in her hair for a second.

"Looks like it!"

"Do you think James is okay?" Beth asked, noting her sister's concerned look as she'd re-entered the kitchen.

"He's probably just worried about his dad," Caspian said. "I wouldn't pry."

Beth nodded, thinking that she should probably send her parents a message or a picture of their holiday. She would mention it to Lee, she decided - although Lee, being the organised one, had probably already done so.

"Have you got any writing done this week?" Caspian asked, as she got up to make another cup of tea and he carefully folded his newspaper.

Beth sighed; "Not much. Now that I don't have a deadline, it's a bit harder to motivate myself, I have to say!"

"You said that last time you started a series," Caspian reminded her. "You'll get there!"

"Always so sure," Beth said with a grin.

"I'm always sure about you."

Lee re-entered the room and made a fake gagging noise, which caused Beth to throw a tea towel at her.

"I said nothing about you feeling your husband up in the kitchen the other night," she said, smiling evilly at her sister, who was turning bright red. "So you can zip it!"

"I wasn't-I-"

"Park!" Holly ran in with one thing on her mind and, grabbing suncream, water and hats on their way out, they set off to oblige her.

*   *   *

After a good hour of pushing Holly on swings, watching her go down the slide and helping her every time she got scared of the high wooden steps, all four of the adults were ready to move on.

"Come on Holly berry," Beth called from the gate. "Lunch time!"

"Swings!" Holly shouted, and Beth looked pointedly at Lee, quite happy to let her be the bad guy. After all, the fun aunt definitely didn't have any disciplining responsibilities!

In the end it was James who swept Holly off the climbing frame in a fit of giggles, and she quite happily exited the park on his shoulders as they headed for lunch.

"I was thinking of getting some writing done this afternoon," Beth said as they waited for their order on metal chairs that were baking hot from the sunshine.

"No worries - I think we'll probably chill by the pool. Holly loves it, and it's so much easier to keep her in the shade..." Lee glanced at James and then whispered to Beth; "Plus I've got an Agatha Christie in my suitcase, so if James plays with Holly in the pool, I'll be quite happy with an afternoon of reading!"

Beth laughed, and although James and Caspian looked over, neither asked why. "Cas?" she asked, presuming he'd heard the beginning of their conversation.

"I might go for a swim then. Are you going to find some well-placed bench to sit and scribble?"

She smiled; he knew her so well. She'd been struggling with this latest series; after finishing her books set in Dartmouth, and then a duet set in Edinburgh, she had decided to start a fresh novel - but the ideas just hadn't been flowing. She presumed she would write a mystery - after all, that was all she had ever written - but she needed something to spark it. And hopefully, a well-placed bench on this beautiful Greek island would kindle her imagination.

"That's the plan!"

*   *   *

With the sun high in the sky and plenty of tourists milling around, Caspian and Beth strolled through the town centre, not really paying attention to much around them but soaking in the atmosphere all the same. Voices in a myriad of accents surrounded them, although Beth only really tuned in to the English words, as she was pretty useless with foreign languages.

She was in search of an appropriate bench, and Caspian had decided to stroll with her, planning to head to the sea for a vigorous swim once she was settled with her notebook.

"I do miss living so close to the sea," Beth said, the closest she'd come in recent months to admitting how much she missed Devon. "I mean, I know Edinburgh has beaches, but it's not quite the same..."

"You mean the Scottish weather's not quite the same!"

Beth laughed; "No, it's not - but then the weather here makes Devon look dreary and cold!"

"It's been glorious," he said. "I'll be sad to leave!"

Beth nodded in silent agreement.

They wandered away from the bustle of the town, until they found a steep hill that looked promising. Impressive views always seemed to have a way of inspiring Beth; they had done in Dartmouth, and in Edinburgh, as she was hopeful they would here too.

Since she'd been writing full time, she was well aware her fitness levels had dropped a little, but she powered up the hill at a similar speed to Caspian, keen to get to the top and see if the perfect spot was to be found.

"Oh!" she gasped; as they reached the brow of the hill, a beautiful vista came into view. A cove, sheltered from the ocean by way of craggy rocks that blocked and calmed the power of the waves. Golden sands and bright blue waters met at one point, and out in the horizon the aqua waters met the cloudless sky. It was an image of perfection - and there, built into similar craggy white rocks at the top of a hill was a bench.

Beth ran to it and squealed, sitting down quickly as if someone might steal it from her.

Caspian laughed, delighted by her excitement. "It is one hell of a view!"

Out of her handbag came that brand new leather journal and several pens - because you just never knew when one might run out.

She stared out to the glittering waters and waited for the inspiration to strike.

"I guess I'm surplus to requirements now!" Caspian said, but he was smiling as he did so.

"I love you!" Beth said with an easy grin. She was distracted from that view by him grabbing her and giving her one of those firework-inducing kisses that made her legs melt and her heart race, before heading off at a jog down the hill. She watched him go, trying to get her mind back on the present and not on how very, very good his lips felt on hers...

Shaking her head, she returned to that view. Little boats were moored at the edge of the cove, and out to sea she spied a large cruise ship, presumably waiting for day-trippers to return. There were a few houses looking out over the water, but all in all it was a much less densely populated area - and to Beth, that made it so much more special.

Watching the water glitter in the glorious sunshine, she couldn't help her mind wandering back to swimming with Caspian under a moonlit sky, when they had first kissed and life had become so much more exciting again. When she'd lived in a city, she hadn't realised what she was missing out on, but when she'd moved to rural Devon shed discovered a love of the beach, the ocean, the freedom of all that space...

And she found Caspian.

As she lost herself in the romance of the moment, she realised one thing with startling clarity: she wanted to be in Devon.

She had known all along, she supposed, that that was where she wanted to end up - but this was such a strong desire to be there *soon* - not when they retired in the distant future, which was one of her fears.

But how would she break that to Caspian? The distance - and her desire to stay in Devon - had caused so many problems when they had been dating. Hell, it had nearly torn them apart permanently more than once. She wouldn't risk that again.

No. She shook her head; they were married. They would not be torn apart. But that did not mean she couldn't broach the subject with him - and see what his reaction was.

She pushed it from her mind, opening that first creamy page and putting her pen to the paper. And as she looked around at those beautiful, deserted houses, and that secret little cove, a story began to take shape. Ideas of the past, of smugglers, and above all of love. Of romance. Of the kind of passion that you only felt once in a lifetime...

Well, they did say write what you know.

CHAPTER TWELVE
Caspian

Caspian pushed himself in the ocean until all he could think about was the water, and the burn in his arms and legs as he kept up the punishing front crawl. He liked to challenge himself, and exercise was no exception to that rule. The crowded beach was full of people sunbathing, paddling and floating around in the water, but a little further out he focussed on swimming length-distance laps and then turning round and doing it all over again. From years of practice off the Devon coastline, he regularly checked to make sure he wasn't going further out to sea than planned, but other than that he focussed. Although it was safer and simpler to swim in their private pool at the villa, for Caspian nothing had the lure of the open sea.

When he began to feel like it was getting to be too difficult, he headed back in to shore and found where he had stashed his clothes and phone. He was surprised to see how late it was getting, and hoped that Beth had managed to find some writing inspiration. He was so proud of how far she had come with what was once her hobby, but he knew she had her doubts when she was finding it hard to come up with a new idea.

As he towel-dried his hair and waited for his energy levels recover a little, he let his feet sink into the white sands and smiled at the memory of Beth doing so on one of their early dates. The beach, the sea; it would always be a place that made him think of her - but especially the beaches in Devon where they had spent so much time.

James's words had been on his mind since they had been spoken. Was he right to keep his feelings from Beth? As much as he didn't want her to give everything up for him once again, he also knew that they'd been burned before by not being completely honest with one another. More than once, in fact. And hadn't he admitted his biggest weakness was a lack of communication skills? Ironic, really, for a publicist - but then it seemed he was better at telling the world someone else's news than he was admitting things to his nearest and dearest.

As he began to walk back to the villa, his legs felt a little wobbly, and he realised he had definitely overdone it swimming. That happened sometimes, he found, when he lost his mind to the activity and took little notice of what his body was telling him. Instead of breaking into a run, he slowly wandered up the hill, and just as he was wishing he had money to buy something sugary to get him home, he spotted Beth. He was about to shout, but she spotted him and ran over, her mouth breaking into a wide grin.

"I was about to call you! I've had an amazing idea for a series - I got so much writing done this afternoon!"

He pulled her tight and kissed the top of her head, laughing as she squirmed away from his still-damp hair. "That's great news."

"Good swim?" she asked, wrapping an arm around his waist as they wandered back through the town. Lee and James had taken the car, and although they could have rung for a lift, Beth seemed to be planning to walk.

"Yeah, lovely," Caspian said, stopping next to a hut selling ice creams. "Can we get an ice cream?"

Beth gave a fake gasp of shock and grabbed her purse, knowing his wallet was somewhere safely in the bottom of her bag. "Not like you, Mr Blackwell!"

"I think I overdid it swimming," he said. "I'm so exhausted. Lee and James won't mind if we're a bit later for dinner, do you think?"

"Nah, they'll be fine. James is cooking - I'll text and tell them we can eat later if they need to feed Holly or whatever."

The benches around were all packed with people, so they took their ice-creams and perched on a wall. The sea was just about visible in the distance, and they watched as the market traders began to pack away, and the restaurants got their outside tables ready for the busy evening trade.

"I wanted to talk to you, actually," Beth said, tapping her foot against a loose stone at the bottom of the wall.

"Oh?" Caspian said, and then decided now was a good as time as any. "I wanted to talk to you, too, actually."

"You go first," Beth said, and although the gentleman in him wanted to insist she start, he thought he was better to get it out.

"I've been thinking..." He paused, licked his ice cream, and tried again. "There've been some redundancies at work. Nothing I think will affect me, but, well... it got me thinking. And I'm doing so much managerial work, and not getting to do the actual work I really love..." His words seemed to be getting more convoluted, but it was hard to get to the point of what he was trying to say. "What I mean is, I've been having thoughts of leaving the business. Of... of setting up on my own." He glanced up at her, squinting against the sunny background. "What do you think?"

"I think if that's what you want, then it's a great idea, of course! You're so disciplined, you be great working for yourself."

He smiled at that; she was always his champion, even when he didn't feel he deserved it.

"And..." He took a deep breath and then pushed himself on. "And we seem so settled now, and this does not have to mean anything changes - I mean, I don't want you to change anything if you don't want to. But I was also thinking that, if I started my own business... well, there's no reason it couldn't be in Devon. If that was what we both wanted."

Beth looked at him, her ice cream melting faster than she could eat it and dripping down her hand. "Is that what you want?"

For a moment he didn't want to answer, didn't want to sway her decision or cause any tension on their perfect holiday... but he had promised when he married her to be honest.

"Yes. It's what I want... but only if it's what you want, too."

And then she broke into the biggest smile, and threw her arms around him, mindless of the ice-cream which ended up half down his back and half on the floor.

"Whoops," she said, but the smile on her face suggested she didn't really care. "That's what I wanted to talk to you about. I want to move back to Devon... sometime before we're sixty."

Caspian felt his heart soar, and in the heat of the setting sun he kissed Beth and felt like nothing truly mattered unless she was there and she was happy.

"I think that sounds like a plan, Mrs Blackwell."

CHAPTER THIRTEEN
Last Night

"I don't know where the last ten days has gone," Lee said, sighing as she sat on the balcony with a large glass of wine and her feet perched in James's lap. "I don't want to leave!"

"I know," Beth said, looking out to the sea in the distance. "I love being warm all the time!"

They laughed, and Caspian placed a rustic-looking pizza on the table in front of them. There was a stone pizza oven built in a corner of the garden, and James and Caspian had insisted they had to try it before they left - and so now, on their last night in this paradise, they had finally got round to it.

"That smells amazing," Beth said, cutting off a section and passing it to Lee so it could be left to cool for Holly. Caspian and James grinned proudly.

"Plenty more coming!" James promised, cracking open a bottle of beer, then offering one to Caspian.

While Holly tucked into her slice of pizza and they waited for the next to finish cooking, they sat and looked out at the spectacular view, enjoying sitting out of an evening in shorts and t-shirts which, they knew, was rarely do-able at home.

"So," Beth said, a smile on her face and one arm stretched to hold Caspian's hand. "We wanted to tell you that we've had a chat... and we're going to see how feasible it would be to move back to Devon."

Lee's face broke out into a smile. "That's brilliant! When?"

Beth laughed; "Hold your horses - we've only just realised it's what we both want. It'll take some time... but we're definitely looking to do it sooner, rather than later."

James clapped Caspian on the back on his way to get the next pizza from the oven; "That's brilliant news, mate." A friendship had certainly grown between the two during their time away that seemed deeper than just the connection they would always share, being married to two sisters.

As they tucked in, they discussed the details a little further, before moving on to other topics: Lee's plans for the cafe this winter - she was hoping to start serving food, although even she laughed at the suggestion that she would be doing the cooking - and Beth shared a few details of the novel that had begun to take shape in her head.

"Have you messaged mum this week? Or dad?" Beth asked as the boys went to retrieve yet another pizza, despite everyone feeling stuffed.

"I sent them both a photo a few days ago," Lee said; "That one we got the waiter to take at the restaurant of all of us. Got an enthusiastic reply back from dad and a slightly cooler response from mum - the usual!"

Beth rolled her eyes; "Sounds like it. I kept meaning to message, but never got round to it!"

"They know you're away, don't worry about it. Besides, have they been messaging you?"

"Dad sent one to say he hoped we had a good time," Beth said. "But no, I haven't heard anything from mum."

Lee sighed; "You know, I don't think I'll ever quite understand her. Very, very occasionally she lets her guard down and I think 'wow, I've totally misjudged her'. And then she does or says something that makes me completely confused all over again."

"I know what you mean," she said. "I see Caspian with his mum - or James with his, even - and it's a relationship I just don't understand!"

Lee glanced over at Holly. "I hope she's not saying this stuff in thirty years' time."

"She won't be," Beth said, an air of certainty to her voice. "You're so much warmer than mum, Lee - no, it's true. I know she doesn't mean to be, but she is cold - she always has been. I love her, but it's true. I think we maybe take after dad more, because I don't think either of us is like that."

"I wonder what she would have been like if dad had never left," Lee said. "I think he really hurt her,"

Beth nodded; "I do too. But he didn't mean to... and we can't live our lives thinking 'what if'."

"No, I guess we can't." She topped up her wine, a little splashing down the side of the glass, and grinned as James offered to take Holly up to bed. "Thank you, wonderful husband," she said, reaching over to give her daughter a big kiss and a cuddle before waving her off to bed.

"He's so great with Holly," Beth commented, helping herself to a glass of wine and savouring the first sip.

"He's a complete natural as a father," Lee said. "Holly never wants me instead of him - in fact, I sometimes wonder if it's the other way round!"

*   *   *

As the night grew later and the wine flowed more freely, the conversation became louder and a little more risqué.

"Let's see," Beth said, picking at the label on the wine bottle as she considered what the next question should be. It had started as a game of truth or dare, but when no-one had really been up for completing a dare, it had instead turned into a truth-telling exercise.

Lee was not sure it was something she wanted to encourage, but a third glass of wine was making her a little less cautious than she normally was.

"Aha," Beth said, a glint in her eye and a wicked smile on her lips. "First times. When - and with who - did you lose your virginity?"

Lee groaned, and Caspian rolled his eyes, but they had come far enough with the game that none of them were backing out. No-one, however, was keen to go first.

"Oh, I'll go," Beth said, leaning forward and whispering as if there was someone to keep the salacious details a secret from. "I was seventeen, and it was with Sonny Johnson, who was in my A-Level drama class."

"Sonny Johnson?" Lee exclaimed, her eyes wide. "I never knew that!"

"Well, you don't tell your big sister everything," Beth said with a giggle.

"Well I never."

"You go!" Beth said, leaning back in her chair and rather enjoying the game she had begun.

Lee blushed, but didn't shy away from the question. "I was eighteen," she said. "And it was a guy on my law degree - Nick, although you wouldn't know him."

"Ah, I think I had heard that one," Beth said, turning expectantly to James.

James shrugged, and although he was still smiling, there was reticence in his eyes. "You'll laugh," he said, with a shake of his head.

"We won't!" Beth insisted.

"Don't force people, Beth," Caspian said.

"I'm not forcing," Beth said with a huff, but she stopped pushing and went to ask Caspian instead - when James spoke.

"I don't mind telling you, but it's not so typical. I was twenty-one... and it was with Lottie. At the time, I thought we would be getting engaged, and married..." He shrugged. "I'd waited until I thought it was right. Of course, I didn't quite predict her leaving me a week before the wedding."

"What a-"

"Indeed."

"Nothing to laugh at," Lee said. "Nothing wrong with waiting for the right person... just that she wasn't it."

"Oh, she most definitely was not," James said. "I'm glad we both realised that before we were married!"

Lee sighed; "I wish I'd realised that before I married Nathan." She rarely talked about her ex-husband, but the wine was making her tongue looser and her brain less of a filter.

"No what-ifs, remember!" Beth said. "Everything's good <u>now</u> - that's all that's important. Now, Caspian, your turn."

"Not much to say," Caspian said. "I was sixteen, we went to the school dance together, one thing led to another..."

"School dance?" Lee asked. "Did you grow up in a fairy-tale?"

Caspian laughed. "Just a small town school!" he said. "Maybe there just wasn't much else to do..."

Beth giggled, and leant back against Caspian's broad chest. "I'm so pleased we're not in secondary school anymore."

"What does that mean?" Lee asked with a chuckle. "We're adults, why would we be in school?"

"Oh, you know what I mean - glad that we've grown up, that we don't have all that school drama, stressing about who's cool and who's not and having crushes on boys... I'm a lot happier now."

"Me too," Caspian said, kissing the top of her head.

*　　*　　*

Somehow the night seemed never-ending, and as it grew later the air stayed balmy and the conversation did not stop flowing. They all knew they would feel it in the morning - which was not all that far away - but for now they enjoyed each other's company and the beautiful surroundings for one last night.

"I do miss home," Lee said, as she and Beth grabbed glasses of water for everyone. "Even though I don't want the holiday to end."

"Me too - although your home, more than mine I think..."

"Well it's a good job you'll be living close again soon, isn't it. I've missed you."

They embraced in the kitchen, a few alcohol-driven tears falling down Lee's cheeks. "I've missed you too!" Beth said, feeling like her one glass of wine had also gone to her head.

"I should check on Holly," Lee said, and Beth looked her up and down and shook her head. Thankfully, James had only had a couple of drinks and so would be perfectly capable of taking care of Holly should the need arise - but the wine had definitely affected Lee the most, and there was no doubt she would wake her daughter up.

"I'll be quieter," she said. "I'll go - you go back outside."

"Best sister ever!" Lee said, tripping through the doorway. Beth rolled her eyes and quietly climbed the stairs. They hadn't heard anything on the monitor, and so she was not surprised to see Holly fast asleep, cuddling a toy rabbit in one hand and sucking the thumb of the other.

She watched her niece, so peaceful in sleep, for a few minutes, before re-joining the party.

"This has been the best holiday ever," Lee was exclaiming as she went back outside, and she smiled as she took her seat next to Caspian.

"Agreed!"

"I think we should make it a regular thing. Or semi-regular, at least. I know we're all very busy people-"

"You more than most," Beth interrupted.

"Well, maybe not for much longer. You've got me thinking. Anyway, we should do it again - next year."

"I'm in," James said, and Beth was pretty sure he'd say yes to anything Lee wanted. She was pleased her sister had found someone who worshipped her in the way she deserved -

someone who loved her and who she loved so fiercely in return.

"Sounds like a plan," Caspian said in his deep voice, and Beth turned to look at him. The moonlight reflected off his glossy back hair and made his smile seem even brighter. She'd found someone too, she thought, who loved her more than she thought was possible - and she loved him back just as much.

"To love," she said, raising her glass, and they all joined her, not caring that the sun would be up soon or that their holiday was so nearly over.

Tomorrow they would worry about packing, flights, getting home, work, and all the things that filled their very busy lives. But tonight was just about happiness; about celebrating love in all its forms. And when they finally turned in for the night - or morning - they all felt intensely grateful for everything they had.

CHAPTER FOURTEEN
Epilogue

It had been five weeks and six days since they had landed back on the tarmac at Heathrow airport, and gone their separate ways; Beth and Caspian on a train back to Edinburgh, and Lee, James and Holly off to their car in order to drive back to their cottage in Devon.

In those five weeks and six days, their tans had faded, and the weak English sunshine had not been enough to keep them looking as bronzed and glowing as they had felt when they had returned. They had gone back to their normal lives as if nothing had changed, with work, and nursery, and writing, and all the other things that fill days and weeks and months.

But so much had changed.

For one, Lee Knight had suddenly realised that she had not had a period since before they had been on holiday. Normally, this might not have triggered any real reaction; she had never been that regular. That's how she'd ended up not realising she was pregnant with Holly until after she had thrown up across the front stoop of a local shop - but then that was a story she tried not to remember.

But for some reason this time, after their wonderful, relaxing holiday away, after opening her heart to her sister and her husband and accepting finally that perhaps she could not be everything, to everyone, all of the time... she had an inkling that this time might be different.

Holly was at nursery, and James at work, and she was supposed to be working on checking the legalities of a will for a local couple with a very convoluted family. But once the thought had entered her head, she was unable to focus, and so instead headed out to the car and drove to the supermarket. Well, actually, she drove to the supermarket in Paignton, a town a few miles away - because she knew that if she were seen buying a pregnancy test in Totnes, the news would somehow get back to everyone she'd ever known - and she couldn't cope with people's comments if she were going to be disappointed yet again.

The whole drive there she tried to convince herself that she mustn't get her hopes up; that like every time she had taken a test in the last year, this one would more than likely be negative too.

She desperately tried to quash the excitement that was bubbling up within her.

Her hands were shaking as she grabbed the first one she saw, not bothering to compare the prices, and rushed to pay at the checkout. She was almost desperate enough to go and take it in the supermarket's toilets, but changed her mind at the last minute. She didn't want to be upset here; she was better off at home, where she would have time and space to recover from the disappointment before James or Holly was home. She probably wouldn't even tell James she'd taken it; he didn't need to know of every disappointment. It didn't change anything.

The journey home seemed to take an age, and by the time she was in the bathroom with the door locked - just in case - she had convinced herself many times over that it would be negative...and then hope crept in that it might be positive.

If the journey home had seemed long, the five minutes waiting for the test to be ready to read was an eternity. Her legs jiggled up and down from where she was perched on the side of the bath, and when her phone bleeped she took one very deep breath, and stood to view the test.

Two lines.

She blinked, sure it was a figment of her imagination. She had spent so many hours staring at tests she had taken, willing a very faint line to be there, announcing she was pregnant. But it had not been.

And now it most definitely was.

Feeling like her legs might melt beneath her, she took the test and her phone and moved to lie down on the bed, one hand on her stomach as the euphoria built inside her. She was pregnant.

It was early days, she knew that, and she knew of all the risks - but the first hurdle was cleared. She was actually pregnant.

When she had found out she was pregnant with Holly, her emotions had been so different. Disbelief, terror, sadness, happiness... such a maelstrom of feelings when she had found she was going to have a baby with a man she had not known for very long. Such a wonderful man, such an amazing dad, so that now...

She felt nothing but pure joy.

It took her a second to realise that her phone was ringing and, in a daze, she pressed answer without even looking at who it was.

"Hello?"

"We're coming home!" The voice was loud and exuberant and very clearly belonged to her sister Beth.

"What?"

"We're coming home! Caspian has handed in his notice, he's got a whole plan for his own business, we're moving back to Devon!"

"Oh Beth," she said, feeling tears rolling down her eyes that she didn't think were wholly due to her sister's good news. "I'm so pleased for you!"

Beth screamed. "I'm so happy!"

"I can tell!"

"Are you all right?" Always perceptive at awkward times, Lee thought with a sigh.

"I'm..." She didn't know what to say, but the word was there on her tongue and although her sister should not have been the first person she told, she couldn't help herself. "Beth, I'm pregnant!"

"Lee!" Beth shrieked, and Lee laughed through her tears and moved the phone away to avoid her ears ringing.

"That's amazing! How far? When's it due? What did James say!"

"Whoa," Lee said. "I found out about five minutes ago... And I really should have told James first!"

"Ah, he'll understand. I'm doing a happy dance, are you doing a happy dance?"

"Yes," Lee lied - but she was grinning from ear to ear.

*   *   *

Five years later...

Beth Knight strolled through the gardens of Greenway, smiling to herself as she looked out over the treetops to the water and Dartmouth in the distance. It had been a tough climb to the top of the garden, but it had certainly been worth it. Caspian, of course, had made it up there before her and without getting out of breath. Behind her, she wasn't sure her sister and James were so convinced the climb was worth it.

"Hurry up slowcoaches!" she shouted with a grin, knowing her sister would be sure to get her back for that one later. No matter how old they got, there was always a little friendly sibling ribbing between them - even though they got on so well.

Lee huffed and glared at her sister. On her back she was carrying little Harry, who was coming up to five years old and had refused to walk once they started up the hill. James had offered to carry him, but when seven-year-old Holly had insisted she had to hold her daddy's hand and nobody else would do, Lee had ended up as the lucky winner.

Beth laughed and stuck her tongue out. "There's a bench up here!"

Eventually the four adults and two children squashed onto the bench, which was partially hidden by trees. Beth had discovered it when she had worked here, and it afforded great views of the water - if you were willing to sit in the shade of the trees.

Lee swigged her water and groaned. "I'm too old for this."

"Nonsense - you're not even forty yet!"

"*Elizabeth*," Lee said, using her sister's given name very deliberately. "You know very well forty is looming over me like an axe. We can't all be young, successful authors who get enough sleep and still look twenty."

Beth rolled her eyes and took her husband's hand. She wasn't too far off forty either - although a couple of years behind Lee, of course.

"Forty's not so terrible," Caspian said with a smile. Flecks of grey had begun to speckle his dark hair, but if anything Beth thought it added to his rugged good looks. Running his own publicity business was stressful, but once he'd established it and felt confident in his staff, Beth had managed to persuade him to take fairly regular holidays, and so the stress hadn't taken too much of a toll on his face.

"Anyway, *Shirley*," Beth said, giving her sister a taste of her own medicine. "You look gorgeous, and well you know it, so stop fishing for compliments."

James jumped in before Lee could respond. "So, is there a reason you've dragged - I mean brought - us up to this beautiful location?" he asked, smiling as Beth shot him daggers for suggesting he'd been dragged.

Somewhere in the banter the children had wriggled off the bench, and were running around the grass, doing funny attempts at cartwheels and covering their clothes in grass stains. It made them all grin, and Beth turned to Caspian, the smile on her face broadening.

"Yes. We've got some news. Caspian and I - we've decided to adopt."

There was silence for a moment as this news sunk it; it was most definitely not expected.

"Wow!" Lee said. "That's great! But how... why...?"

"We've been discussing it for a while," Caspian said. "And we've actually got all the paperwork lined up. We're ready to start a family - but we decided what we want most is to offer a family to someone who doesn't have one. Maybe more than one someone if it works out - we'll see."

"So we're going to adopt a child, not a baby," Beth said, looking to her sister for approval as she so often did. "We're waiting to hear back on one possibility..."

Tears were in Lee's eyes, and she reached over Caspian to give her little sister a hug. "I think that's wonderful, Beth," she said, full of sincerity after their joking. "Caspian... so wonderful. And so exciting to add to the brood of cousins these two have got!" James's brother and sister had been blessed with several children, and family Christmases now spread over several rooms - and resembled a child's birthday party. Since the death of James's father two years previously, it had felt like there was a hole in the gatherings that couldn't quite be filled - although the children did try very hard to fill it with noise and mess!

Beth smiled; "It feels right," she said, and she gave Caspian's hand a squeeze. She had been so nervous in case her sister had thought it was a silly thing to do... although she didn't really know why she'd worried. Of course Lee would think it was a good idea.

"It's beautiful here, isn't it," James said after they had sat for a long while watching the water and the children running around and squealing.

"There's so many places in Devon where I just seem to feel at peace," Beth said. "I loved when we lived in Scotland, but nowhere has ever felt so right as here."

"I know what you mean," Caspian said.

"Well I've never really left," James said with a grin. "So that must be a ringing endorsement!"

"Imagine if Lee had driven somewhere else, all those years ago, and not Totnes!" Beth said, although her smile faltered a little at the thought.

"I'd rather not," Lee said, and James's arm tightened around her as they watched their children beginning to argue about the rules of whatever game they were playing. Holly would inevitably win; she had something of the lawyer in her, James always said.

"No," Beth said with a sigh as she rested her head on Caspian's shoulder and let her mind drift back to sparkling kisses in the icy sea. "I think you're right. Everything worked out for the best, in the end, don't you think?"

Lee gave her hand a squeeze and nodded. "The very best."

*   *   *

I can't quite believe I've come to the end of 'The South West Series'! When I started writing Lee and James's story, I planned it to be a one-off Christmas novel. Now, I feel like I know these characters so well, and it has given me an opportunity to fall in love with the places all over again! I wanted to take them away from Devon in this last instalment, so they would realise what they really missed about the place.

I never like to say never, but I'm not currently planning on writing any more in the South West Series. However, I have another series already in the works and may write a short story with these characters in the future! To stay up-to-date with my publishing, you can join my newsletter here: http://tiny.cc/paulinyi

Thank you so much for choosing my stories to read. I really hope you've enjoyed them and it would be brilliant if you could review this book on Amazon; it really does make the world of difference. You can also get in touch by emailing me at rebeccapaulinyi@gmail.com

Until next time - happy reading!

__Acknowledgements__

Thanks to germancreative for her wonderful work on my covers. Thanks to my husband, for always giving me time to write, and my mum for always being desperate to read it!

Printed in Great Britain
by Amazon

61176991R00070